I'll Always be Your

Daughter

I'll Always be Your Daughter

A Fable for Mothers & Daughters

CAROL LYNN PEARSON

GIBBS SMITH
TO ENRICH AND INSPIRE HUMANKIND
Salt Lake City | Charleston | Santa Fe | Santa Barbara

Revised Edition
14 13 12 11 10   5 4 3 2 1

Text © 2000 Carol Lynn Pearson

Published by
Gibbs Smith
P.O. Box 667
Layton, Utah 84041

1.800.835.4993 orders
www.gibbs-smith.com

Designed by Sheryl Dickert Smith
Printed and bound in China
Gibbs Smith books are printed on either recycled, 100% post-
consumer waste, FSC-certified papers or on paper produced from
a 100% certified sustainable forest/controlled wood source.

Library of Congress Cataloging-in-Publication Data

Pearson, Carol Lynn.
  I'll always be your daughter : a fable for mothers &
daughters / Carol Lynn Pearson. — rev. ed.
     p. cm.
  ISBN-13: 978-1-4236-0761-8
  ISBN-10: 1-4236-0761-9
  1. Mothers and daughters—Fiction. I. Title.
  PS3566.E227 I25
  813'.54—dc22
                    2009027635

There was a beautiful strong oak tree who spent her days enjoying the sunrise and the breeze and the birds, and especially the clouds that formed patterns in the sky.

One morning an acorn fell from one of her branches, and she watched in great satisfaction.

"Ah," she said. "A Daughter! That's what I have always wanted, a Daughter." She looked down at the acorn and smiled. "Hello, Daughter!"

"Hello, Mother," said the Daughter.

"This is good," said the Mother. "You will be here close to me, and I will watch over you. You will grow to be just like me and will be my Daughter forever."

Soon a squirrel came scurrying along and picked up the acorn and dropped it a little ways away.

"Oh!" said the Mother in surprise. "If you are there and I am here, will you still be my Daughter?"

T his is good," replied the Daughter. "The sun feels warmer when I am not in your shadow. I think I can grow better now. And, yes, Mother, even though I am *here* and you are *there*, I will still be your Daughter."

*T*he Daughter grew and began to look more and more like her Mother. The Mother was pleased and loved to tell stories of the things in the world around them.

"See, that cloud looks very much like an eagle, don't you think?" said the Mother.

"Oh, it does," said the Daughter. "And I love how the light reflects across the water on the little pond with the swans."

"What little pond with the swans?" asked the Mother.

$\mathcal{J}$ust there, past the hill," said the Daughter. "Perhaps you can't see it from where you are. It's lovely."

The Mother craned her trunk and looked and looked, but she could not see past the hill. "Oh, dear," she said. "If you can see a pond with swans and I cannot, will you still be my Daughter?"

"This is good," said the Daughter. "For now I have things I can tell you. And, yes, Mother, even though I can see the pond with the swans and you cannot, I will still be your Daughter."

A drought came and there was no water for them to drink. Day after day, the Mother and the Daughter grew more and more thirsty.

"I can bear it for myself," cried the Mother, "but not for my Daughter. I will pray for rain."

She prayed and she prayed as she watched her Daughter become dry and thin. But no rain came.

"I am sorry," she moaned in despair. "Even a Mother's prayers are not heard! If I cannot change the world for you, will you still be my Daughter?"

*B*ut your prayers are heard," said the Daughter. "This is good. My roots press deeper and deeper into the ground where it is wet. If I did not have to hunt for drink, I fear I should fall at the first storm. And, yes, Mother, even though you cannot change the world for me, I will still be your Daughter."

*B*efore long, a fierce wind came, and the branches of both the Mother and the Daughter swayed and creaked. The Mother leaned as far as she could lean to protect the Daughter, but some of the tender young branches of the Daughter were bruised and broken.

"Oh, you are hurt!" said the Mother sadly. "How can I bear to see you in pain? If I cannot protect you from the wind, will you still be my Daughter?"

$\mathcal{T}$his is good," answered the Daughter. "The broken places tell me I am alive, and now I feel. Some growth has been pruned, but new growth is coming. And, yes, Mother, even though you cannot protect me from the wind, I will still be your Daughter."

The wind became a gentle, happy breeze, and the Mother said, "Oh, listen to the melody our leaves sing with the chirping of the robin in her nest. It is the chime of a thousand small bells."

"That is your melody, Mother," replied the Daughter. "It is a lark that nests in my branches, and the song we sing together is a whistle and a laugh."

"Oh!" said the Mother as she listened carefully. "So it is. But if you sing a different song than I do, will you still be my Daughter?"

"This is good," said the Daughter. "I can listen to your song and you can listen to mine. Together our melodies make a symphony. And, yes, Mother, even though I sing a different song than you do, I will still be your Daughter."

The days and the months and the years moved on, and one day the Mother looked up and said, "Oh, my! How you have grown!"

"Yes," said the Daughter, very pleased with herself. "From you, Mother, I learned to stand as tall as I could stand."

The Mother looked at her admiringly. Then, hesitantly, she asked, "But if you are taller than I am, will you still be my Daughter?"

"This is good," said the Daughter. "Now I can watch over you and try to protect you when the wind blows. And, yes, Mother, even though I am taller than you are, I will still be your Daughter."

One day an acorn fell from one of the Daughter's branches, and the Daughter smiled. "I know what that means!" she said. "A Daughter who will grow to be just like me!"

"Well, not exactly," corrected the Mother.

"Ah . . . ," said the Daughter, thoughtfully. "But, Mother, if I did not grow to be just like you, are you disappointed?"

*T*he Mother looked up at the beautiful strong tree that stood beside her, silhouetted against a crimson sunset. "Oh, no," she said. "You are you, and you are better than I ever dreamed."

"And if I am a Mother, too—"

"You will always—"

"Yes, I will always, forever and always, be your Daughter."

"This is good," said the Mother.

"And your friend," added the Daughter.

"Ah!" said the Mother. "A friend! That's what I have always wanted!" She looked up at the Daughter and smiled and said . . .

H ello, Friend!"